MONSTER WORLD

Book One

1.   The Red Diamond

By Priya Grewal

Chapter One

Dekrov awoke from his slumber and stretched his arms. He had been asleep for three days. He slowly sat up in bed and looked around his cottage. The cottage was made out of wood. There was a pleasant dining room in the middle of the cottage and a fireplace. He had a few vases of flowers around the cottage to make the cottage look pleasant. Aside from that there wasn't much else he bothered putting in his cottage. He had a small kitchen with a kettle and surfaces to prepare food. He had food in his cupboards and teabags. Dekrov got out of bed and went to look in his mirror above the fireplace.

Dekrov turned his head to the side as he looked in the mirror admiring his face. Dekrov was a monster demon. He lived on a planet called Monster World. Dekrov had a triangularish face with large horns on the top of his head. He had very sharp teeth and beige colour skin. Dekrov had moved out of his parent's home around 100 years ago. He had two siblings who he didn't bother much with. His two brothers were already married with children. Dekrov didn't want to get married yet. He wanted to have a good time living by himself. He visited his parents once every few years when they pestered him to. Monster World was full of different monster demons. There were around a trillion different species on the planet. All species had females and males in it. The history of how Monster World had come to be was lost many generations ago. Apparently, the myth was that they were made by all powerful beings called gods. The monsters didn't know what these supposed gods looked like. The tale said that the gods had made all the monsters in monster world. For what purpose no one knew. Over the generations the tale merely became a myth. No one ever finding or seeing evidence of any such gods existing.

Oh well, Dekrov thought to himself still looking at his reflection in the mirror.

Who cares how we came to be, Dekrov thought to himself smiling. *I love monster world.*

Dekrov loved his life on Monster World. He enjoyed meeting up with his mainly male friends and having a good time playing sports and games. He loved going to the Alehouse and drinking beer and sitting around with his friends. He had a few close female friends.

Dekrov was topless as he looked in the mirror. He grinned at himself and flexed his muscles and growled in the mirror. Satisfied with his appearance, Dekrov put a black garment on followed by a black cloak. After breakfast he would head to the ale house to sit around and drink with whichever companions were already at the ale house.

Chapter Two

Dekrov stood at the bar in the ale house waiting for his beer to be served. His favourite tavern was called 'The Long Mead.' The bar tender, a one-eyed green cyclops called Rotu was serving today.

"Thanks," Dekrov said to Rotu, smiling appreciatively as he took his first sip of beer. Dekrov turned around and leaned against the bar as he drank his beer.

Suddenly he got wind of the conversation 3 monsters were having in a booth in the ale house. He listened as the voices travelled over to him.

"That's not real," he heard a monster he was acquainted with called Falaro say. Falaro had a large horn in the middle of his head and many eyes.

"It is," a monster he recognised as Jaraz said.

A third monster called Bezrael sat and listened not saying a word.

"It's an artifact made by the gods!" Jaraz said excitedly.

"What gods, there are no gods!" Falaro bellowed.

"Well, where did we come from then?" Jaraz repiled.

Falar and Bezrael responded with silence, not knowing how to answer the question.

"What is this artefact then?" Bezrael asked.

"It's cut into the shape of a red diamond," Jaraz continued. "It is said to have all the powers of the gods inside it."

"All the powers of the gods inside it?!" repeated Bezrael, transfixed by the conversation.

"Yes! Yes!" Jaraz responded excitedly. "Imagine what one could do with it! You could rule the WHOLE world! Make everyone bow to you in worship!"

"So, where is this diamond?" Falaro asked.

"I don't know," responded Jaraz.

Dekrov chuckled to himself quietly tuning out of the conversation as the three monsters squabbled between themselves.

He turned around to face the bar again. Suddenly, the cloaked figure sitting next to him on a stool lifted their hood off their head.

He saw he was standing next to a female monster. She had purple wavy hair and deep purple eyes to match. She had two small horns on her head.

Dekrov nodded his head in greeting to her. The monster demoness grinned a wide sharp toothed grin.

"Hello," she said. "My name is Sarqual. I'm a succubus."

"Hello," Dekrov responded. "My name is Dekrov. I'm one of the horned demon folk. The ones with really large horns," he added. "I haven't seen you around here before."

"That's because I haven't been around here before," Sarqual responded, smiling.

"Touche," Dekrov responded.

"It really is real, you know," Sarqual said, smiling slyly.

"What is?" Dekrov responded, glancing at the deep purple eyes of the succubus.

"The diamond," she responded as if it was obvious.

"Oh whatever," Dekrov said. "I don't believe in mumbo jumbo."

"I can show you, if you don't believe me," Sarqual smiled.

"Okay," Dekrov responded.

"Follow me," Sarqual instructed.

Dekrov downed the last of his beer and followed Sarqual outside of the tavern.

"Sit by me," she said, sitting on a large grey boulder.

Dekrov sat on the other large grey boulder beside her.

Dekrov's eyes widened as Sarqual produced a magical bubble in between her hands.

"You have MAGIC!" Dekrov cried.

Magic was extremely rare in monster world. Only a few witches who lived in a nearby village had access to any. They had a limited supply. If you had something to offer them, they may give out a little. It was usually just used for a little bit of mischief like destroying one's plants in their garden if a monster had a grudge against them and not being caught.

"You're not a witch,"Dekrov gasped. "You're a succubus."

"I'm part witch on my grandmother's side," Sarqual responded happily.

"So, I have access to a little bit of magic, gifted to me by the witches for being kin," Sarqual explained. "Now look," she ordered.

Dekrov's eyes widened as he looked at the scene in the bubble.

There in a sandy desolate brown sand and concrete area was a red diamond dug underneath the sand. It glimmered a shiny red. Dekrov couldn't believe it.

"What does it do?" he asked, shocked at the sight of it.

"Everything they said it can do," Sarqual told him, eyes gleaming.

"All the powers of the gods? So, the gods are real?" asked Dekrov.

"Yes," Sarqual responded. "That's where the magic comes from. No one knows where the gods are though," she quickly added.

"So, what do you say?" Sarqual asked. "Do you want to go and find it?"

"And do what with it?" Dekrov asked, eyes gleaming with excitement.

"Rule the world of course," Sarqual said.

"How?" Dekrov said. "By magicking in possessions they want? Jewels etc?"

"Noooooooooo," Sarqual said viciously. "We just use the magic to forcefully make them bow to us and serve us, with no effort on our part. Using the magic!"

"Oh," Dekrov said, beginning to laugh. "Okay, I'm in. How come you want me to be your partner in finding it?"

"The place where it is rumoured to be is mistrustful of women. So, I need a male companion. I came here because the rumour reached my village. It was said it was being spoken of at this tavern. So, I turned up to see if I could get any information. Luckily, those three monsters were there talking about it. You look strong and sturdy and tall. So, looks like you're a good fit for a partner," Sarqual explained.

Dekrov liked being called 'strong and sturdy and tall.' He didn't see what risk there was in going along with finding the object.

"I'm in," Dekrov confirmed, pledging himself to the mission and hopefully all great power.

"Excellent," Sarqual grinned. "First, we need to visit a friend."

"And who's that?" Dekrov asked.

"An ancient witch who lives in the witch village," Sarqual responded, happily.

"Let's go," she said.

Chapter Three

Dekrov followed Sarqual as she led the way to the witch's village.

"What's the name of this witch then?" Dekrov asked.

"Horanio," Sarqual responded.

"What do we need the magic for?" Dekrov asked.

"Well, I can't disguise us as the species of the planet the diamond is located on. I don't have enough magic," Sarqual told Dekrov.

"Which planet is the diamond in?" Dekrov asked.

"It's on a planet called Earth. The species there are called humans. They have a head and body like ours but look different. They call the time it is the 12th century over there. They have magic there as well. Some there practice it," Sarqual explained.

"We need the magic to get us there and for us to have human disguises. I don't have enough magic to do either. Horanio can disguise us as a male and female human. She can only do the same gender, hence why I still need a male!" Sarqual told Dekrov.

With all explained, Dekrov said, "Well, lead the way then madam."

A short while later Dekrov and Sarqual reached Witch's Village. The sign stating, "You are now in Witch's Village" had fallen off its hinges.

As the pair entered the village, evening approaching, they saw a lot of witches having a good time outside of their cottages. Dekrov could hear happy cackling and see small fires lit in front of many of the cottages. The witches seemed to be standing around the fires having a good time nattering along with one another.

Dekrov hadn't spent any time in the village before. The witches had different coloured faces with warts on. Some had green faces, others blue, others purple. Some were flying on broomsticks happily. Many had on their black witches' hats.

Dekrov followed Sarqual, trying not to show any fear of the witches. He felt a little scared of the witches due to their magic and what they could do to a being with the magic. He tried not to make eye contact.

"We're here," Sarqual told Dekrov, stopping in front of a cottage door with the word 'Welcome' on the letter box in black handwritten letters.

"Don't say anything unless she asks you a question," Sarqual advised Dekrov. "She doesn't know about the mission. I'm just going to say we want to visit the human world."

"I won't say a word," Dekrov declared, lifting his hand in promise.

"Okay," Sarqual replied. She turned around and knocked on the door three times.

A minute later Dekrov heard a croaky voice say, "Who is it?" from the other side of the door.

"It's Sarqual, the succubus," Sarqual replied.

The voice on the other side paused a moment. "Just be a minute," the voice responded.

A minute later with Dekrov and Sarqual standing on the doorstep for a moment longer, Horanio opened the door.

Dekrov looked at Horanio's face. It was green with only two warts. Less than some of the other witches.

"Oh," Horanio said, eyes widening looking at Dekrov, as she ushered the pair in.

"Who is this fellow?" Horanio asked.

"This is my friend, Dekrov," Sarqual explained. "We're going travelling together."

"Oh right," Horanio replied. "Do sit down," Horanio said pointing at two chairs that were in front of a black cauldron.

"Would either of you like any tea?" Horanio asked.

"Just a flying visit," Sarqual responded.

"Oh, okay then," Horanio said, walking to the armchair on the other side of the cauldron and settling herself into it.

"What can I do for you both today?" Horanio asked, professionally.

"I need enough magic for both of us to take on a disguise to look human," Sarqual said. "We also need some travelling magic to get us to the planet Earth."

"Planet Earth, you say?" Horanio asked. "That's an interesting location to go and explore. Any particular reason you're going there?" Horanio asked the pair.

"Just for the experience," Sarqual lied. "We heard that the people there also have access to magic, so thought it sounded like an appealing planet to go and visit."

"Okay then," Horanio said, not questioning them any further. "You know I can only do same gender disguises not opposite ones."

"Yes, that is fine," Sarqual responded.

"And what do you have to give me in exchange?" Horanio asked, clasping her hands together.

Dekrov watched as Sarqual unattached a small bag from her belt and pulled out a beautiful ring with a large blue ruby in the middle of it.

"Ah," Horanio exclaimed, looking at the ring. She stretched her hand out and Sarqual placed the ring in the middle of the witch's palm.

"It is rather lovely," Horanio stated, eyeing the ring from every angle.

"Anything else?" the witch asked.

Sarqual reached into her small bag again and this time pulled out a large silver necklace with different coloured rubies encrusted into it.

"Ahhh," Horanio said, happily.

She reached out and Sarqual handed her the necklace.

"This is lovely!" Horanio squealed happily. "I shall wear it to the next Solstice festival."

Sarqual let out a small sigh of relief.

"Very well," Horanio said, putting the items in a chest of drawers.

She settled back into her armchair.

"Give me your hands," Horanio instructed Sarqual. Sarqual reached out with her hands. The witch took the two hands and closed her eyes. Dekrov watched as both pair of hands glowed purple.

"There you are," Horanio said a moment later, letting go of Sarqual's hands.

"And your friend?" Horanio inquired.

"Yes, him too," Sarqual responded.

Oh, goody! Dekrov thought in his head.

He stretched out his hands uncomfortably as he saw the witch's green hands clasp his.

She closed her eyes again. Dekrov watched as this time his hands glowed purple. A slight feeling of warmth entered his arms and hands.

The witch let go a moment later. Dekrov was glad the physical contact moment was over.

He looked at Sarqual.

"Well, that will be all," Sarqual said to the witch and Dekrov.

Sarqual stood up and Dekrov followed.

"Thank you so much, Horanio. We will be on our way," Sarqual bid farewell to Horanio.

"Oh, do come again some time! And bring your friend!" Horanio followed them to the door, letting them out.

"Thank you," Dekrov said to the witch as he exited the cottage.

"Oh, goodbye," the witch squealed happily, shutting her door a moment later.

Dekrov followed Sarqual as she walked away from the cottage. She turned a corner.

She stopped abruptly and began cheering.

"Yippee!!" she squealed delightedly.

"We've got the magic! One step closer to the all-powerful diamond!" she cheered.

Dekrov laughed, joining in on the fervour.

"What next?" he asked, after cheering for a moment.

"Let's get out of the witch's village and find an empty path. We can switch into our disguises using the magic and take off from there," Sarqual instructed.

"Lead the way," Dekrov responded, a feeling of excitement building up inside of him.

Chapter Four

Dekrov followed Sarqual out of the Witch's Village. She followed a pathway that led into the woods. When she reached a cluster of trees, she stopped.

"Here will do," she told Dekrov.

"So, what first?" Dekrov asked, looking at Sarqual.

"Let's change into our disguises," Sarqual instructed.

"How do we do it?" Dekrov asked.

"Just think *make me human* inside your head and you will change," Sarqual instructed.

"Okay, you go first," Dekrov requested.

"Fine," Sarqual replied.

Sarqual closed her eyes. All of a sudden, a split second later her form began changing. Dekrov watched amazed as her horns and purple hair and eyes disappeared to be switched into a face he had never seen before. Sarqual now had a light brownish skin colour with two blue eyes, a nose and a mouth. She now had yellow hair.

Hmm, us monsters are way better looking! Dekrov thought to himself in his head.

"Your turn," Sarqual ordered, once her transformation was complete.

"Fine," Dekrov imitated. Dekrov thought the words *make me human* in his head. A split second later he felt a warm feeling in his body. He watched dismayed, as he watched his hands and arms change form.

"Great," Sarqual said, once the transformation was complete.

"Can I look in a mirror to see what I look like?" Dekrov asked. Sarqual rolled her eyes.

She shoved her hand into her little bag attached to her belt again and took out a compact hand mirror.

"Here," she said moodily.

Dekrov took the mirror. He opened it. He chuckled as he looked at himself. He now had a pale skin tone with black hair and green eyes. He laughed looking at his wavy black hair.

"Do you prefer me like this or with my horns?" Dekrov asked Sarqual.

"What do you think?" snapped Sarqual. "With your horns obviously."

Dekrov laughed again.

"Ditto!" he exclaimed.

"Okay, that's enough messing around," Sarqual ordered. "Let's get going!"

"Waiting for your command, madam," Dekrov said.

"Let's join hands. When I say so, think the words *take me to earth* in your mind and then we will be transported there," Sarqual instructed.

"Righteo," Dekrov responded. He reached out his hands and Sarqual clasped them in hers.

"Okay, after three..." Sarqual ordered. "One, two, three...".

Dekrov thought the words *take me to Earth* in his mind. A moment later he felt a cold wind rise from the ground around him. He saw himself and Sarqual get caught in a mini tornado. The grey tornado swirled around them for a few moments. Then, as the tornado began to die down and fade away, Dekrov looked around him.

He had been transported with Sarqual to a different planet.

He looked around him. They were standing on a green hill. He could hear sounds of laughter from a distance away. He saw that down the hill there was some kind of town. With the human faces talking loudly. He saw a woman with a cup of beer in her hand.

Looks like the humans like ale houses too, Dekrov thought to himself.

"We're here!" Sarqual whispered, excitedly. "Let's go and find our diamond."

A grin widened on Dekrov's face.

Chapter Five

"What do we do first?" Dekrov asked Sarqual, walking down the green hill with herself.

"We have to find a man called Merlotto," Sarqual told Dekrov.

"I checked with my limited magic to see what we had to do when we got here," Sarqual explained. "There's a man in his 70s with white hair called Merlotto. He doesn't know that the diamond is real but he has heard a story about its location. We have to find him and find out the location and then we can go and get it!" Sarqual exclaimed, excitedly.

"He lives in this town called Greenfield," Sarqual informed Dekrov.

"That's why I've transported us to this place in particular. Apparently, he hangs around a human ale house here called *The Five Moons.*"

Sarqual took a circular object out of her bag attached to her belt.

"What's that for?" Dekrov asked.

"It's my magical compass," Sarqual explained. "It tells us what direction to go in."

Dekrov glanced at the compass. He saw the words *walk straight* appear on the compass and then *turn left.*

Dekrov left Sarqual to look at the compass and followed her.

A few turns later, Sarqual stopped and said, "Here we go!"

Dekrov stopped abruptly in front of an ale house. He read the sign saying *The Five Moons.* There was a shape of a crescent moon beside it.

Sarqual smiled. Dekrov followed her into the ale house. He had a look around, nearly forgetting about his human disguise. Sarqual and Dekrov both blended in, no one giving them much notice. Sarqual got the odd glance from the human males.

No horns anywhere! Dekrov thought to himself, amused.

Dekrov glanced at Sarqual. She was still looking at the compass. It was still instructing her. He peered over her shoulder to read what it said.

The words *the man you are looking for is sitting in the last booth on the right formed* on the compass.

Sarqual and Dekrov both looked up. A man with white hair and a moustache was sitting in a booth a frothy liquid in front of him in his cup. He was talking to one of the bar tenders who was standing next to the man's booth, making conversation. The man Merlotto looked quite jolly.

"Here we go!" Sarqual said triumphantly, snapping shut the compass and placing it in her bag again.

"You just say hello and nod happily," Sarqual whispered to Dekrov. "I'll do most of the talking!"

"Okay," Dekrov agreed. The less work he had to the better, he thought to himself.

Dekrov and Sarqual both in their human disguises, walked over to the man Merlotto's booth.

Chapter Six

"Hello," Sarqual smiled at Merlotto.

"May we join you?" she asked Merlotto.

Merlotto looked surprised for a moment and glanced at Sarqual and then Dekrov.

After a second he said, "Sure join me, young people!"

The bartender looked at Sarqual and Dekrov as they sat down opposite Merlotto.

"Can I get the two of you anything?" the human male asked the pair.

"Just two beers please," Sarqual requested. She fished around in her bag and produced some coins. She put it in the bartender's hands.

"Be back with your beers," the bartender said.

Dekrov smirked. They didn't have coins in Monster World. *She's thought of everything, even brought coins with her used on this planet!* Dekrov thought to himself.

"So, you from around here?" Merlotto asked Sarqual and Dekrov.

"We're not from too far away," Sarqual answered. "We're just travelling around at the moment. Exploring the country."

"Ah well that's a grand idea! Right age to do some travelling when you're young!" Merlotto responded jovially.

The bartender returned with the beers. Dekrov and Sarqual both said thank you simultaneously. The bartender returned to the bar.

"We heard a story on our way here. About a diamond said to have the powers of all the gods. Myself and my friend here really enjoyed the story!" Sarqual told Merlotto.

"Oh yes! The diamond story! I heard it in my youth too! Said to be in the Sahara desert in the story!" Merlotto exclaimed.

"I loved that story when I was younger! I don't practice magic myself!" Merlotto told them both. "But there are practitioners of magic in this town! They call themselves Elders. Most of them are in their 70s! I don't know where the magic comes from though! How it came to be! I'm not too bothered about magic! I enjoy myself at the Ale Houses! I have a good time! Don't need magic to entertain myself!" Merlotto told them both.

"The Sahara desert?" Sarqual asked. "Where is that?"

Merlotto frowned for a second.

"Oh, it's around Egypt. That kind of area. Where the pyramids supposedly are. Kings buried with treasures in their tombs so they say!" Merlotto told them cheerfully.

"Well!" Sarqual said, glancing at Dekrov. "We best be on our way. We just popped in for a quick drink and rest," Sarqual told Merlotto.

Sarqual grabbed her cup of beer and swallowed the whole drink in seconds.

Dekrov imitated her.

"Oh, okay!" Merlotto replied, looking a little disappointed. "Well, the best to both of you! Best wishes on your travels!" Merlotto said, raising his cup of beer to them both.

"Thank you for your company," Sarqual said, standing up and getting ready to leave.

"It's been a pleasure," Sarqual added.

"Bye," Dekrov said to Merlotto.

Merlotto nodded and the pair headed to the door of the Ale house. Dekrov didn't say anything until they had left the building.

Then he grinned at Sarqual.

"You genius you," Dekrov whispered into Sarqual's ear.

"Yippeeeeee!" Sarqual cried.

"We're nearly there. One more step to complete universe power!" Sarqual celebrated.

Dekrov chuckled happily.

"Where shall we depart from?" Dekrov asked Sarqual.

"Let's get back to the top of the hill so no one sees us," Sarqual responded.

"You're the boss," Dekrov said, following Sarqual back up the hill.

When they reached the top of the hill, Dekrov turned to Sarqual.

"Shall I think take me to the Sahara desert in my head to be transported there?" Dekrov asked Sarqual.

"Ah, you're getting the hang of magic now!" Sarqual responded.

"Just think *take me to the Sahara desert in or near Egypt,*" Sarqual told him. "Just so we have a more specific location."

"Let's hold hands again," Sahara said grabbing Dekrov's hands.

"After three again," Sarqual instructed. "One, two, three..."

Dekrov thought the words in his head and felt the warm rush of the power in his body again. Again, the pair were caught up in a mini gusty tornado.

Seconds later, as the tornado fell away from the pair, Dekrov looked around at the surroundings.

The sun was setting and the sun cast a glow on the sand so it looked a reddish colour.

Dekrov inhaled a sharp breath looking at the vast size of the desert.

Sarqual pulled her compass out again.

"Let's get our diamond," she said.

Chapter Seven

"Okay," Sarqual said excitedly. "Looks like it's not too far from this spot. The compass is coming up with specific instructions."

Dekrov glanced at the compass.

Keep walking straight, the words formed on the compass.

Dekrov and Sarqual kept walking straight for around two minutes.

They were both still in their human disguises.

The words changed on the compass.

Turn right and start walking straight again.

Dekrov made a face. He was getting confused trying to remember his right from his left. He didn't usually have to think about it in Monster World.

At least Sarqual's here to copy, Dekrov thought to himself. *I don't have to think about remembering my right and left too much.*

Dekrov carried on walking straight next to Sarqual. Suddenly, she stopped.

Dekrov looked at the compass.

You have reached your destination, were the words now written on the compass.

Dekrov gasped.

"And now?" he asked Sarqual.

Sarqual closed her eyes. She started turning back into her monster self again. Dekrov watched as her purple horns and hair and eyes returned. He glanced at his hand. He too was turning back into a monster.

"Oh, goody!" Dekrov exclaimed happily.

Next, Sarqual started moving her mouth, chanting words in silence.

"What are you doing?" Dekrov asked.

"Getting the diamond, ssh!" Sarqual said. "I'm using magic!"

"Oh," Dekrov fell silent, feeling powerful and sturdy again in his monster form.

He watched Sarqual.

A few moments later a purple circle formed around Sarqual. Dekrov heard a sound like stones were shifting out of place under the sand. Dekrov gasped as the red diamond popped up from underneath the sand. It was glowing red and brilliant.

"It's here," Dekrov whispered slowly and dramatically, feeling stunned.

Sarqual opened her eyes. She looked at the diamond and grinned.

She grabbed the diamond greedily.

"What now?" Dekrov asked stunned, not sure what to do next.

"How do we take over the world?" Dekrov asked.

Sarqual started cackling gleefully.

"I'm going to unleash the magic!" Sarqual exclaimed trimuphantly.

"How do we use the diamond?" Dekrov asked.

"We just need to command it and it will do what we say, as all magic works," Sarqual advised.

"I want to take over every planet in existence," Sarqual stated.
"The monster ones and the human one! I'm going to say to every inhabitant in every universe there is to bow to us both or else we will enslave them," Sarqual declared cackling.

"Enslave them?" Dekrov asked, starting to jump around ecstatically.

"Yes, it means I'll put heavy loads of materials in front of them and whip them while I force them to try and move it!" Sarqual declared.

"That's if they refuse to bow to us!" Sarqual added.

Dekrov grinned conspiratorially.

"Let's do it," Dekrov grinned maniacally.

Sarqual commanded the diamond.

"Diamond," she said, "amplify my voice so every inhabitant on every planet that exists can hear me! Make them forcibly bow to us!"

The diamond glowed red and it travelled from Sarqual's hand and began floating in the air as it activated.

"INHABITANTS OF THE UNIVERSE!" Sarqual shouted. "YOU HAVE BEEN TAKEN OVER!!! MY NAME IS SARQUAL. I AM A MONSTER DEMON! YOU WILL ALL BOW TO ME OR BE ENSLAVED!"

Sarqual's body started floating in the air too, along with Dekrov's.

"Ahem," Dekrov spluttered, nudging Sarqual with his elbow.

"YOU HAVE BEEN TAKEN OVER BY 2 MONSTERS! I AM A SHE DEMON! MY FRIEND'S NAME IS DEKROV! YOU WILL BOW TO BOTH

OF US OR BE ENSLAVED FOR ALL OF ETERNITY! WHIPPED UNTIL YOUR BACK AND HANDS BLEED PUSHING HEAVY MATERIALS AROUND FOREVER!" Sarqual shouted.

"Diamond," Sarqual commanded the diamond. "Make it so mine and Dekrov's faces are enlarged in outer space and in every sky so every inhabitant can see us, both of us!"

Dekrov laughed and laughed.

"Amplify my voice too diamond," Dekrov commanded the diamond, as they both sailed in the air above the desert sands.

"I AM YOUR MASTER NOW!" Dekrov declared to every inhabitant across the universe.

"MASTER DEKROV AND MISTRESS SARQUAL! REMEMBER OUR NAMES WE WILL RULE OVER YOU ALL FOREVER!!" Dekrov screamed.

"Mistress?" Sarqual asked.

"Just go with it," Dekrov shrugged.

"Let's watch them all," Sarqual said.

"Diamond, show us every town on every planet!" Sarqual asked the diamond.

A magical globe formed and the diamond started showing the two monsters the scene of every town in the universe. The red magic was forcing everyone to bow forcibly.

"Diamond," Dekrov commanded. "Put statues of me and Sarqual up everywhere!

"Woohoo," Sarqual screeched, doing somersaults in the air.

Dekrov and Sarqual watched as colossal statues of the pair of them began to be erected in every town square across the universe. Their faces were in every sky in every town in every country in every planet across the universe!

"The magic will stop forcing you to bow once you say, SARQUAL AND DEKROV I pledge to worship you both forever as King and Queen of the Universe, from this day onwards for eternity," Sarqual commanded.

Dekrov and Sarqual watched as the monsters in monster world, the inhabitants on every planet there was, ones the pair had never even heard of, started to move their mouths and pledge loyalty to themselves. They watched as every human on planet Earth began pledging themselves to the pair one by one until the magic stopped forcing them to bow.

The monsters and humans both quickly fled into their cottages and shelters once they had pledged.

"WE DID IT!" Sarqual shouted.

"We've taken over the entire universe," she screeched in delight.

Dekrov joined hands with Sarqual and the pair screeched and danced in glee, sailing through the air of the desert sands.

Chapter Eight

It was one week later.

Sarqual lounged on a throne eating some fruit she had her monster servants deliver to her.

When Sarqual and Dekrov were done making every inhabitant alive in the universe bow and pledge to worship them forever, Sarqual had conjured a massive black castle for her and Dekrov to enjoy themselves in, as King and Queen of the universe. She had conjured two large thrones for themselves to sit on.

After taking over the entire universe, Dekrov and Sarqual had gone walking around the human and monster towns making every citizen bow to them in person. They entered their homes.

Sarqual laughed happily thinking of them all stuttering as she threatened to enslave them again and them all getting on their knees and pledging worship again.

Dekrov linked her arm afterwards smiling and murmuring his thanks after every house they visited.

Aside from their walking around, the streets were all desolate. Empty. Everyone stayed hidden indoors.

Sarqual and Dekrov had asked for volunteer servants from Monster World to wait on them hand and foot in their castle.

They threatened to whip them all again if no one volunteered.

They took around 15 monsters to be their servants in their palace.

They cooked for them and served the pair all their meals and drinks. Sarqual and Dekrov had had a wonderful time eating massive meals and drinking from golden goblets at a large dining table she had conjured for the pair of them.

She had conjured them both crowns as well as Queen and King of the Universe.

She was glad that she had brought Dekrov along with her. She had a lot of fun taking over the universe with a companion.

She remembered that she may have not even got the story out of Merlotto if she didn't have Dekrov as a male companion.

Poor Merlotto, Sarqual thought to herself. *Whimpering along with the rest of them asking himself what has he done.*

He didn't dare say a word to us about it, Sarqual thought.

"Are you thinking about Merlotto again," Dekrov laughed. "You've got that small smile on your face again."

"Yes," Sarqual smiled laughing. "It was just so funny when he looked at us aghast and didn't swear or curse at us about the diamond."

"Poor Merlotto," said Dekrov happily. "He had no idea that the story about the diamond was real."

Dekrov flung his leg over the arm of his throne and ate happily into his peach. He drank happily from his golden goblet.

A monster came hurriedly up to Sarqual saying, "The fruit you ordered your majesty."

"Okay," Sarqual said conjuring up a table between her throne and Dekrov's, using the diamond. The small monster had a large bowl of fancy fruits in his hands.

"Put it on the table and be off with you," Sarqual barked.

Dekrov started laughing again.

All of a sudden, the lights in the castle started blinking. Sarqual frowned looking up at the chandelier.

A moment later the ground started to shake.

Out of nowhere, tons of witches and human males teleported into the castle room.

"NO!" shouted Dekrov.

Sarqual watched as Horanio came to the forefront.

"Oh, not Horanio," grumbled Dekrov. "I hate Horanio."

"Quiet," Horanio ordered.

Next, a man with a long white beard stretched out his hand and the red diamond flew out of Sarqual's pocket and into his hand.

"NOOO!" screamed Dekrov. "It's those Elders Merlotto was on about. The men in their 70s with magic."

"That's right!" one of the Elders said.

Then, the witches and Elders all started chanting together.

"We banish you Sarqual and Dekrov into a stone underground prison to be chained up for all of eternity, with only each other for company. We bind you both from ever wielding any kind of magic again to harm any species in this universe," the witches and Elders chanted together.

"NOOOOOOOO!" screamed Sarqual.

A tornado formed around both Dekrov and Sarqual, this time not for the better.

"NOOOOOOOO," they both screamed together.

Seconds later, the pair were chained to the ground and in a stone underground prison of blue rock.

"YOU WILL NEVER BE RELEASED FROM YOUR PRISON," a deep voice rumbled. "Humanity and the monster planets will all be restored, never to be harmed by your evil again."

The voice said no more.

Dekrov and Sarqual tried to pull their chains out of the ground.

The chains didn't budge.

"NOOOOOOOOOOOOOOOO!" both screamed and spat repeatedly into the air again, with only their echoes to reply.

Chapter Nine

Dekrov and Sarqual had both collapsed onto the ground moments later, giving up on trying to pull their chains out of the ground.

"Oh, why?" Dekrov started to moan. "Why did I have to listen to you? Why couldn't I have just been happy with my cottage."

Sarqual looked up.

"Oh, whatever," she hissed. "Too late for that now. Don't blame me!"

"Who else is there to blame?" Dekrov moaned. "I wish I never clapped eyes on your purple eyes and little horns!" Dekrov moaned.

"Well, it's not like I'm thrilled about only having you to stare at for the rest of eternity," Sarqual barked back, defensively.

"OHHHHHHHHHH, WHYYYYYYY!" Dekrov moaned, howls filling the air.

Dekrov put his head on the ground, wishing he hadn't taken the bribe of being worshipped by the entire universe forever.

He looked at Sarqual hating her face and hating her for ever coming into his life.

His howls filled the air again as he stared at Sarqual, the only face he would ever see again for all of eternity.

No food, no drink, no cottage or Alehouse for himself to have a good time in anymore.

Sarqual had nothing more to say.

She stared gloomily back at Dekrov, knowing she had got her come uppance.

THE END

Printed in Great Britain
by Amazon